FALCON

CYBORG RANGER

CHRISTINE MYERS
CLARISSA LAKE

Book Cover by Christine Myers

Illustrations by Deposit Photo Royalty Free Images

Contents

Chapter One

Cyborg Ranger Falcon Rader paused to receive a message from his internal computer as he left the house to make his rounds. "Yeah!" he shouted as the words hit his emotional center. His genetic mate finally replied to his request to meet him.

He had been made to fight the war against the Mesaarkans but an avatar of his genetic mate, the female he would love was planted into his mind before he was born. Or in a cyborg's case, before he emerged from his nurturing tank where he had been grown from an embryo.

Until now his genetic mate had been an unfulfilled promise. Now a hundred years later what was another week? Only a week ago, she became real.

Before then, she had been an avatar of the female he would love planted into his mind before he was born. Or, in a cyborg's case, before he emerged from his nurturing tank where he'd grown from an embryo.

In the year since his return to Earth, Falcon had spent most of it in old Nebraska and Kansas. Taking back towns and villages from mob bosses, he stopped them from confiscating the best crops and crafted goods for themselves. They were mere annoyances compared to the overlords in California and the dishonest town officials in Texas. By his assessment, they only needed peacekeeping protectors from the awakened Chicago cyborgs.

His plains states had fared better than those with heavily populated megalopolises. The Mesaarkan dropped their bombs on the most heavily populated cities of the world. The plains states were left mostly intact. Yet, the residents were not left unscathed by the infrastructure damage throughout the country.

Even before protectors arrived, a team of cyborgs traveled around collecting DNA profiles to help cyborgs find their genetic mates. They had found Falcon's mate in southeastern Kansas.

The Genetic Mate Project notified him and sent her his request to meet her right away. Raya Monroe had volunteered to be included in the database. The Project confirmed she received his request. Why did she take so long to answer?

Every second of the past week seemed to tick by excessively slowly. Had Raya changed her mind? Would she now deny him?

Falcon already decided; he wasn't taking 'no' for an answer without meeting her face to face. What made her hesitate? Was it his greeting vid?

Other females found him attractive, but they weren't for him. It would be so much easier if he could just pick a mate. But it was programmed into their genes and into their minds. They could only feel attraction and procreate with their genetic mate.

His was thirty-six-year-old Raya Monroe. The sound of her voice awakened emotions he'd never felt before. He looped her response vid every few minutes after examining it frame by frame, noting every nuance in her facial expression as she spoke.

Some might say he was obsessed. He could thank his programmers for that. Uniting with his genetic mate had been figuratively held in front of him as the ultimate payment for fighting the enemy battle after battle, year after year. Sometimes, he'd been so tired and broken he could barely face another day.

Then his internal computer would open her avatar to lift his spirits. At the same time, his nanites forced the production of feel-good hormones. Briefly, he could imagine what his life could be when the fighting was over.

The promise of her carried him through battle and months of recovery from injuries that would have killed normal men.

Falcon's memories flashed through his mind in a couple of strides on his way to his personal flyer. It'd cost him two years' pay plus shipping from Phantom. It got him back and forth across his territory twice as fast as the sky cycles they'd been issued for the job.

No flyers had been manufactured on Earth since before the war. The cyborg rangers and protectors knew they were lucky to have the sky cycles. If it ever happened, it would take at least a decade or more to get a facility up and running to build such vehicles on Earth again. Only cyborgs and some overlords could afford them.

In one respect, that was good. Restoring law and order was easier without all the petty tyrants having a speedy means of escape. The bigger tyrants were limited in the territory they could control because advanced modes of transportation were in short supply.

Flying at high speed toward southern Kansas, Falcon was happy he got his flyer in time for the trip to meet his genetic mate.

It was midmorning when Raya finally decided to meet the cyborg—Falcon, who she'd learned was her genetic mate a week ago. The cyborg Dagger and his mate Chloe who collected her DNA profile seemed so happy together. Chloe assured Raya; she would love having a cyborg mate. Dagger clearly worshiped the ground she walked on, so to speak.

Raya had an occasional lover since her parents died far too soon. Modern medicine might have saved them if they'd had access to any. Those supply chains dried up shortly after the Mesaarkan attack. It got lonesome living and working the farm all alone.

At the end of the day, it would be nice to have a man to share a meal with and to hold her in his arms until she fell asleep. Sometimes, she just wanted to get laid. That's what made her join the gene pool for a cyborg mate.

But did she really want a male around all the time to get in her way while she was trying to get things done? Cyborgs were military-groomed and trained. When she first got Falcon's introduction vid, her first impulse was to respond immediately.

He was so handsome, and his voice was outright sexy. But he looked like he was barely twenty-five. Raya knew she was still attractive but thought she looked her age. Would he want a woman that much older?

She was working in the vegetable garden when she heard a soft whine in the sky. It was similar to the sound Dagger's flyer made. Then she saw it. A minute later, it was hovering over the dirt road in front of the house and landing.

Raya watched, clutching her hoe handle, as the door slid open and a tall, lean, yet muscular male stepped out. He was dressed in black cargo pants and a tight-fitting black t-shirt, wearing a white hat with a circled star on the front.

Her mouth fell open, and she forgot to breathe as he strolled toward her. Everything about him exuded alpha male, and he was gorgeous. His gaze found hers, and his lips curved into a self-assured smile. However she had thought this would go down, Raya never expected to feel such a profound attraction to him.

He looked every bit as young as she thought from his greeting vid. Suddenly, she couldn't think why it was a problem. The cyborg was looking at her as if she already belonged to him. If she could reason at that moment, Raya might conclude she had been his since she had opened his vid and looked into his midnight blue eyes.

It was hot standing in the sun, but that wasn't the cause of the heat that suffused her body or the clamoring of her lady bits for his attention.

The man stopped and stood before her, holding his hands out to her.

Raya dropped her hoe handle and hastily shed her leather work gloves, dropping them on the ground to put her hands in his. He was so tall she had to look up at him to see his eyes.

"Hello, Raya. I'm Falcon Rader, your cyborg."

"I-I didn't expect you to be so young…."

"How old do you think I am?"

"Twenty-five?"

"Ninety-seven," he deadpanned. "More than old enough to appreciate the beauty of an 'older' woman." Then he smirked and winked.

"You can say that now, but what about when I am older, grey and wrinkled, and you still look twenty-five?"

"That won't happen. The nanites I share with you in my body fluids will prevent that. You will even look younger in time."

Raya smiled at him, knowing he was telling her the truth. It seemed clear he was determined to become her mate.

"May I kiss you?" he asked, politely waiting for her to answer.

Her eyes went to his beautiful mouth, and she could only nod. Raya could no longer think of a single reason why this could never work.

Still holding her hands, he bent and lightly pressed his mouth to her parted lips. As a frisson of attraction raced through her body, Falcon pulled her against him and deepened the kiss.

Raya gave in and simply held on to him. She made a mewling sound as his tongue took over her mouth. His body was all taut, hard muscle, and his chest felt delightful plastered against her breasts.

Raw desire surged through her body, and she vaguely realized she'd known this would happen as soon as she'd seen the vid. It had been a long dry spell between lovers. The last one tried to steal her horse.

That was not how things worked when a woman took a cyborg mate. He stayed and became a permanent part of her life. He valued her above all else, and that intrigued her.

"Well, what do you think?" Falcon asked when he'd parted his lips from hers.

"We should probably go inside out of this hot sun," she muttered.

Chapter Two

Falcon nodded and released her, offering his hand. As she took it, he waited for her to lead him into her dome-style ranch house. It was a sleek, minimalist dwelling of aerated concrete, built before the war, powered by solar arrays and a windmill. He visually assessed the three main rooms in a split second before returning his attention to Raya.

He took her face between his hands and stared into her eyes. "Raya, you are my genetic mate, the only female I will ever desire. My only chance to love and be loved and maybe have children someday. You are the woman I have been groomed all my life to love. No one else…. Only you."

He paused to kiss her softly. "I'm not some newly awakened newbie. I fought ninety-seven years for the promise of you. I am an old man in a young body. In my eyes, you are the most beautiful woman in the world because you are meant for me. Can you turn me away because you think I look too young to be your mate?"

Unable to speak, she shook her head against his hands. She covered them with her smaller ones and turned her face to kiss his palm. Not knowing what to say, she pressed her body against his and hugged him. It wasn't that he looked younger. Despite everything she learned about cyborgs, she feared he would reject her.

Raya knew she wanted him the moment he stepped out of his plane. "I'm sorry," she said against his chest. "I didn't mean to make you think that. That was my own shortcoming talking." She leaned back and looked up at him. "I've had men nowhere near as handsome as you who didn't think I was good enough or pretty enough…."

"Raya," he said, her name with a reverence that stunned her. "They weren't made for you. I am. I am your cyborg, and I want you more than my next breath."

There had been little enough pleasure in her life the last few years. Why deny what they both wanted out of some perception of propriety? How long was proper? One day? Three days? A week?

Cyborg marine rangers were the best of the best. They fought longer and harder than anyone else in the war. He was hers; he said as much.

This man came here to be her mate for life. It was a done deal. She signed up for that when she consented to put her DNA profile in their database. With her body clamoring to have him inside her, she couldn't think of a reason not to fuck him. That was the pheromones working on both of them because of their genetics.

She didn't love him yet, but she would if he stuck around long enough.

"And I want you," she whispered, knowing she had to say the words before he would act. Falcon had spent his whole life fighting for the promise of love. How could she deny him?

Nothing prepared her for what happened next. He scooped her up in a bridal carry and headed toward the hallway that led to the bedrooms. Hers was the only one open. Setting her on her feet, he removed his hat and put it on her dresser. Turning back to her, he ran his fingers through her honey-colored hair and smoothed it over her shoulders. He gazed at her with a look of wonder that pulled at her heartstrings.

No man had ever looked at her with such devotion or desire. Yet he didn't move, so Raya stepped back and unbuttoned her shirt. She looked him in the eyes with a compassionate smile as she pulled back the sides, shaking it off her arms and letting it fall to the floor.

Untying her hand-sewn halter bra, she let that fall to the floor, baring her breasts that were just too full to go without support. "Your turn."

Falcon seemed frozen to the spot. His mouth opened, and he licked his lips. "So beautiful," he said hoarsely before pulling his shirt untucked from his pants and off over his head.

"Yes, you are," Raya said with a smile. "You've never done this before." She realized.

"Only in virtual reality…. I know what to do. I won't hurt you."

"I know…. God, you're gorgeous…." She couldn't help smiling at his expression when she said that. "I want to breed with you. Right here, right now."

She followed her declaration by untying her pants' waist and pushing them to the floor. She stepped out of them and the homemade sandals on her feet. Her undergarment tied at the waist followed them to the floor.

Falcon groaned, unable to take his eyes off her female body. Raya stood with her shoulders back, arms at her sides, letting him look his fill. When he still didn't move to touch her, she opened the hook-loop closure on his pants, freeing his engorged cock.

He growled, ending with a groan as she took him in her hands and stroked his silky length. Raya hunkered down and kissed the tip, licking a drop of precum from the end. As she started kissing up his length, Falcon picked her up with his hands under her arms and put her against his chest, wrapping her in his arms.

"I won't last if you do that, sweetheart," he rasped.

Raya put her legs around his hips and crossed her ankles because she could no longer touch the floor. She held him around his shoulders and kissed his neck from the base to his ear.

"I'm ready if you need to take me now…" she whispered. She had been wet for a while; she'd never known a man this sexy without even trying to be. Her nipples were tight peaks, and her clit throbbed as she pressed both against him.

Kissing her passionately, he worked his feet from his boots and shed his pants. He never broke the kiss as he tipped them onto the bed with her beneath him.

Raya reveled in his kiss, the sensual dance of their tongues stoking her arousal. She let him know with her caresses that she cherished him.

Knowing how much he wanted her and all he had been through; she couldn't deny him any pleasure she could give him. She soon understood that giving her pleasure was as important to him.

When his lips parted from hers, he dropped little kisses over her face before exploring the rest of her body with his lips, tongue, and hands. Her breasts were aching for attention when his lips closed over her left nipple. Falcon nibbled and sucked until she writhed and moaned while caressing his head.

Sweet, generous male. His cock was so hard it must ache, yet he pleasured her at length. He dragged his talented lips and tongue over every inch of her body before he found his way to her pussy. He feasted there, licking and sucking until she wailed in ecstasy, unable to remember ever coming so hard.

He wasn't kidding that he knew what to do.

Wiping his face on his arm, he lay over her, his erection lengthwise against her cunt.

"That was amazing!" Raya assured him, caressing his face and pulling him in for a kiss. "I still want you to fuck me... breed me... however you want to say it.'

"How about now?" He lifted his hips, and she spread her legs wider, drawing up her knees to fit him between her thighs.

Falcon drew his cock head up and down her slick, then inserted it at her entrance. After a couple years of celibacy, he was big, and she was tight. Pushing into her slowly, he pulled back and pushed in several times until he was fully sheathed inside her.

"How do you feel?"

"Like you belong here." She smiled and stroked his cheek with her fingers.

"Because I do." He smirked and kissed her. Watching her face, he pulled back and thrust into her.

Raya sighed her pleasure and stroked his back, noting a few scars on his otherwise smooth skin.

Thrusting in and out of her several times, watching her expression, Raya sensed that he wanted her to keep her eyes open as he fucked her. She kept up with him until he pounded into her so fast, she couldn't. Then she held on and let him take her as he needed.

She wanted to please him more than she wanted her own pleasure. While she didn't know what he went through in the war, she'd learned of atrocities many cyborgs had suffered. Initially, they were treated like machines instead of enhanced humans with dampened emotions. Treated as expendable, many died horribly or were captured and tortured by the Mesaarkans.

Their creators brainwashed them with the promise of love and their own families to inspire them to fight with all their strength and endurance to save the Federation.

What surprised Raya was that the long hard fucking Falcon gave her was exhilarating. She couldn't remember ever feeling such joy in a man's arms. She came three times before he finally poured his seed against her womb.

And when he lay spent in her arms, she held him preciously close. How had she ever thought she could turn him away?

Chapter Three

Falcon lay on his side, head propped on his hand, watching Raya sleep. They had spent the last two days in bed since he arrived. Even though she was physically healthy from working her farm, she required more rest than a cyborg. She had said fucking him was a full-body workout.

He loved that she met the challenge so enthusiastically. Raya was more than worth waiting for, and he was eager to learn everything about her. He'd learned some from their pillow talk. It seemed easier for her to be intimate with her body than her mind. He could only guess that came from previous rejections.

Falcon had seen the longing in her eyes when she first saw him. Yet, she had used his youthful appearance in an attempt to reject him before he could reject her. He wanted to kill those males who made her think she was unworthy of their attention. Other than stamina, he couldn't ask for more in a lover.

She was tender and enthusiastic; she had made him feel she cared for him in their short time together. He had fucked her long and slow, teasing her on the brink of orgasm late into the night. She had reveled in it as much as he did.

They said the mating pledge when they finished. "I am yours, and you are mine as long as I breathe," Raya said back with tears in her eyes. Happy tears, she'd said.

Falcon could understand after the hard life of a cyborg marine ranger. Raya had brought joy into his life like he had never known. It was time for them to figure out how their lives would mesh together.

An hour passed when she started to stir and wake. She smiled at him when she saw him watching her, stroking his arm.

"I'm real, and I'm still here."

"I'm glad. I would have been so disappointed to wake up and discover it was all a dream."

"It was no dream, my lovely Raya. I am yours, and I want no other."

"Neither do I."

They were both still naked from the night before. Falcon was wholly tempted to take up where they left off in the wee hours, but he knew Raya had chores to tend.

"I saw that gleam in your eyes," she laughed happily. "We have to leave this bed today. I have work to do."

"And I will help you. We have much to talk about."

Raya nodded with a slight frown.

Falcon reached over and smoothed her brow with his fingers. "No frowning. Nothing to worry about, just things we need to decide together."

The two showered and dressed with only a short dalliance in the shower. Afterward, Raya made them scrambled eggs and toasted homemade bread. Her kitchen was by no means state-of-the-art. She had an ancient refrigerator and a stove that ran on gas from a well on her property.

They had stopped using them long before the war. Still, Raya's ancestor brought it back into the house after the bombings knocked out public utilities. While no bombs fell on Kansas, communications were knocked out before the attack was over. Unlike the current population in the cities, most of the plain's states knew there had been an attack.

While she cooked, she told Falcon where things were, and he took the opportunity to get out dishes and utensils to set the table.

"From the air, I saw a lot of open farmland surrounding your home. Is any of it yours?"

"Most of it, but I don't have the means to work it. I just have a personal garden combine," she said. "My nearest neighbor has equipment but wants the land for himself. He says a woman alone doesn't need all that land. He plants and harvests my fields closest to his land."

"Does he compensate you for the use of your land?"

Raya laughed. "He asked what I was going to do about it. He did hint that we could work something out if I was nicer to him."

Falcon's expression darkened. "Who is this man? I think I need to have a talk with him."

"Nelson Waters. His family has been on the land probably as long as mine has. Since before the war, anyway. I haven't talked to him since he made me his sleazy offer. I didn't like him as a kid and don't care much for him now."

"My next question is, do you want me to come and live with you? Or do you want to go someplace else? My only preference is to be with you," he told her earnestly.

"I hoped you would want to live here. My family is gone. My parents are dead, and my younger sister left ten years ago. I don't know if she is dead or alive. Jenny said there was no future for her if Luke left. So, she followed him when he left. I always hoped they would come back."

"And you want to be here if they do," Falcon concluded. "With the scarcity of fast transportation, maybe she settled someplace too far to travel."

"I thought of that, too. After Dagger and Chloe brought me the com-tablet, I checked regularly to see if he had a code, but he didn't. She doesn't even know that Mom and Dad passed away."

Falcon could see that Raya was upset about her missing sister. "I will see what I can discover while making my rounds."

"Oh, I almost forgot that you are law enforcement here."

"I will have to be away sometimes. We have a criminal organization running a protection racket out of Weshokan that needs to be shut down. I got word that they have even threatened to take children from their families who can't or won't pay."

"Will you be away long?"

"No more than a few days at a time. I won't stay away from you more than I have to. ...And I'll stay in touch. I would get you one if you didn't have a com-tablet."

"You don't have to worry about me. I've been working at this place alone for the last six years. ...But I will surely miss you after the last two days." Raya smiled at him, blushing.

Falcon grinned, came around the table, and bent to kiss her. "I know I will miss you, my mate. But I'm not ready to go back full-time yet. I need to do more recon on the ground first."

Raya smiled at him and glanced back at the table.

"I don't have a dishwasher, so let me clean these up, and we'll go out and see what state things are in."

Falcon helped gather things from the table and then watched how she wet the dishes in the sink and soaped a small rag with bar soap. She swiped it over the plates and silverware, rinsed them under hot running water, and stowed them to air dry on a wire rack over the sink.

Raya started chores hours later than normal, but the last two days had been more than a little unusual.

It was another hot, humid summer day, and it looked like it might rain. As they walked outside, Raya said, "The biggest job this time of year is weeding the food garden. The garden combine plows them under between the rows but I must pull or dig them from between the plants. I have four goats and a horse in the pasture. The three nannies have babies. I'll start milking them again when they're starting to wean. I have a dozen chickens that forage. I just have to collect the eggs."

She was carrying the egg basket. Falcon walked at her side with his hand resting on the small of her back.

"How much land do you have?"

"Just short of a thousand acres. Waters has a point that I can't work it. Probably half our lands have reverted back to grass prairie within decades of the alien attacks. The robot combines that tilled the land and harvested the crops failed when communications were lost, and our AI net failed."

"It's been back up for about four years now. Distribution of com devices just hasn't caught up yet," Falcon said. "If we can find a machine intact, maybe the Enclave has a tech that can connect it to the new AI system."

"I have plenty of pasture land to grass feed cattle, but I can't process them. Even processing one cow, I don't have cold storage for that much meat."

"Is that what you really want to do?" Falcon wondered, trying to discern if that were important to her.

"Personally, no. I have enough to do just growing my own food and keeping the stock I have. I don't think I have eaten beef since I was a kid. Keeping the goats is a lot easier, and I use them mostly for milk to make cheese and soap. I eat mostly chicken, eggs, and vegetables. I manage to grow just enough wheat to make flour for bread, then I have to cart it to my neighbor's farm to get it milled. That's where my horse Suzy comes in."

"I can help you with all that if you let me," Falcon told her. "I amassed a sizeable fortune in credits fighting the war for so many years. If we can source them, I can afford to get the equipment you need."

"That's sweet of you, Falcon. There are some things I can use." She glanced up at him with an affectionate smile that heartened him. "Since we are staying here, you should figure out what you want your role to be here on the farm."

Chapter Four

Falcon stopped them and turned to face her. "My most important role here is to be your mate… to love and support you …take care of you, and make sure you have everything you need… whether it be to help with the work or breed you senseless. I have waited my whole life to be with you."

He cradled her face between his hands and kissed her lips tenderly, passion lurking under the surface. When he lifted his lips from hers, Raya saw the same look in his eyes as the previous night. She caught her breath in a soft gasp as she reflected on what she felt lying beneath him while he fucked her ever so slowly.

Falcon gave her a sexy smirk and caressed her cheek. "I want you again, too." He dipped his head and dropped a kiss on her nose and her forehead.

"That was incredible… and wonderful. I never dreamed it could be like that."

"I did. I think that dream kept me alive more than a few times. I believed if I could stay alive long enough, I would experience it."

"I'm glad you did." She smiled at him, and he rested his forehead against hers.

"I would kiss you again, but then I'd need to take you inside that barn and breed you before we even start chores."

"Then I guess I'd better back away." She laughed. "Because, my handsome cyborg, you are way too tempting." Raya backed away, her eyes sparkling with humor.

With her egg basket hanging on her arm, she took his hand and led him to the pasture to check the goats and the horse. The third nanny had twin kids sometime during the two days she hadn't been to check on them. So now, she had eight goats and could milk again in several weeks.

She said, watching the goat kids frolic, "One thing I've missed for a long time is my dog. She used to keep watch over the goats and run off varmints from the hen house, but she died last year. I don't get anywhere to find one."

"I've seen them around in my travels. I'll see if I can find you one."

"That would be great."

Then, her old horse Suzy whinnied and trotted up to greet her. She nickered and let Raya rub her muzzle, then turned to assess Falcon. The mare sniffed him, and he stroked her neck, talking softly to her.

"I'll get you some carrots while we are weeding the garden," Raya told her as they headed for the chicken coop. Opening the door behind the nesting boxes, she started picking eggs from all the boxes except one.

"What about that one?" Falcon asked curiously.

"She's my incubator. That's how I replace the ones that become food. They should start hatching any day now." With eight eggs in the basket, she closed and latched the access door and headed for the garden shed.

"What do you know about farming?"

"After learning you were my mate, I studied the history of farming and the weather patterns in this area." Falcon named off the primary crops grown before the war, the growth cycles, and preparations for planting them."

"Okay, a lot. How about weeding a vegetable garden?"

"I have images of vegetable plants and common weeds in my database. Since you don't have a bot, I expect we will pull weeds by the roots or use a long-handled tool to dig them out."

"You probably know more than I do. I learned on the job when I was old enough to dig in the dirt." Raya had led him to the tool shed near the garden. She went inside, set the egg basket on a shelf in the shade, and chose a pointed hoe for Falcon.

He looked puzzled momentarily when she handed it to him but didn't get one for herself. "Yours is still in the garden." He remembered.

"So far, I have finished about a third of the rows. It's about all I can do in a day."

"Together, maybe we can finish. This is a pretty large garden."

"I take vegetables to town, trade for other things, and preserve the rest."

When they got to the garden, Raya checked her gloves for bugs before she put them on. She'd left them on the ground

40

overnight, and she didn't want any surprises. Falcon suggested he start at the far side, and they could meet in the middle. Even though she was acclimated to the summer heat, she had to stop after an hour as it got even hotter.

Falcon hardly seemed bothered by the heat, but he could regulate his body temperature better than a normal human. However, he immediately noticed that Raya was on the verge of heat exhaustion, even with her wide-brimmed hat.

"Raya, let's go back to the house and get some water. We can come back at dusk when it's cooler and finish."

"Yes, I was just thinking, I've had enough of this heat. Normally, I would have started much earlier before it got this hot." She gave him a teasing smile. "But somebody kept me up late."

"Is that a problem?" Falcon stepped into her personal space, looming over her teasingly.

"Ut uh. I liked it. A lot." She put her arm around him and pressed her cheek against his chest. Oh, yeah, she was falling fast. How had she ever thought she could send him away?

Raya was also surprised that he was this flirty and fun. He seemed so happy. But why wouldn't he be? He realized his lifelong dream. It still seemed more than a little surreal that she was it.

Falcon put an arm around her and started walking toward the tool shed, pulling her along with him. Returning their tools, Raya grabbed the basket of eggs before they crossed the overgrown lawn to the house. He made sure that Raya drank a sufficient amount of water, then he suggested a shower to cool off.

Even before she started undressing in the bathroom, Raya knew that would happen. Falcon took her in the shower before they even turned on the water. He could do that because he was strong enough to easily hold her against the wall while they fucked.

"I love how you make me feel, Falcon," she told him between kisses afterward.

"What about me?" he growled. "Do you love me?"

She gave him a tender smile and caressed his face. "Yes," she whispered. "I didn't think it could happen so fast. Awesome sex doesn't hurt, but it's more than that. I love being with you," she told him honestly.

"These have been the best days of my life," he murmured, nuzzling her ear. "So many cyborgs haven't found their mates; I wasn't sure I would find you. I almost went out of my mind waiting for your answer to meet me."

"Oh, Falcon, I am so sorry I put you through that…."

"I would have come anyway…."

"I wouldn't have turned you away."

"But you tried."

"Not very hard."

"True."

"But you're still very hard."

Falcon nodded. "Again?" He drew back and thrust into her hard.

"Yes, please," she groaned.

Afterward, they showered, and Falcon carried Raya to her bed for a nap. He lay with her until she fell asleep, pulled his clothes back on, and went outside to finish weeding the garden.

While he worked, he went on the AI net and ordered a garden bot from Phantom. Getting it could take up to a year, but it would save time for other things. He wanted as much time with her as possible before he returned to work, and Raya didn't need to worry about the food garden.

He could afford to have food brought in to meet their needs, but that wouldn't set a good example for community members. The monetary system was being rebuilt, but most people in the western territories didn't have credits in the system. They had no money. People who needed goods or food had no digital currency to pay. They traded goods or services.

The Enclave was working on a system to reintegrate these exchanges into the monetary network. They would broker the sales of goods and services and assign a value to the system.

Before that, he and the other cyborg rangers needed to eliminate the criminal elements running some towns and cities. So far, Falcon had only found that situation in a few in his jurisdiction.

Weshokan was the worst, but it was nothing compared to what Max and Stalker faced in California. Whatever human trafficking was happening in this territory, it seemed local. No alien slavers were involved.

The cities and towns without such problems had strong local governments with their own enforcers to keep the peace. Enclave would send economic advisors to help re-establish trade and their monetary system.

Falcon wished he could be done with it already. When he accepted the job, it seemed like a good way to learn to function in a society where most people were non-cyborgs. It also gave him something to do while waiting and hoping he would find his genetic mate.

Now he had; it would take as much willpower as he could muster to get in his flyer and head out to do his job. His hover plane was too flashy for some places he was going, but the cycle fit in his flyer's cargo compartment.

Falcon knew from his fellow rangers that leaving her would be the hardest part. For that reason, he delayed it as long as possible. No amount of time delay would have made it any easier.

Chapter Five

Four weeks later, Falcon flew his sky cycle to Weshokan. He stashed it on the city outskirts in an abandoned block building and cloaked it. No one else could fly it without his thumbprint and code. But it was small and light enough for a harnessed horse to drag it away.

Instead of his ranger hat, immaculate cargo pants, and standard issue t-shirt, he wore shabby cargo pants with tears and an ill-fitting dingy white t-shirt with badly scuffed work boots. He carried a semi-automatic projectile pistol at his hip with extra clips on his belt. The topper was a battered brown leather outback hat. He had a shotgun in a sling on his back with a row of loops filled with extra shells.

Falcon's size and muscular build made him look formidable. He looked like some kind of enforcer but not a lawman. He had talked it over with Raya and decided to use looking for her sister as his cover story for who he was and why he was there. He wanted to assess the situation before revealing he was a law enforcer.

Weshokan was the closest city, so Jenny Monroe and Luke Sanders could have gone there. Raya wasn't too hopeful that he would find either of them. She knew they both could have been dead for years.

It was just over a hundred miles from Raya's farm to Weshokan, so they could have made it there on horseback in a week or so. After the bombings, many people lost contact with friends and loved ones due to the shutdown of worldwide communications.

The satellite array had been restored for a few years, but the comms distribution was still limited. That couldn't happen until the cyborg rangers and protectors rooted out the tyrants and their gangers.

Falcon didn't have to go far into the city before he came upon a couple of thugs menacing a couple offering vegetables for trading in their front yard. One held them at gunpoint, while the other took most of the produce from the table and stuffed it into a large sack.

"How are we supposed to live if we have nothing to trade?" said the male.

"Not our problem. We let you slide the last two times. Mister Gordon will punish us if we don't deliver."

There was also a basket of eggs on the plank table, and the bag man picked those up too.

"Come on, don't take all the eggs. We were getting flour for them. We haven't had bread in weeks," said the woman.

"Take it up with Mr. Gordon. Consider yourselves lucky we don't take the chickens, too."

"How are we supposed to live if you take all our best stuff. What about our children?"

"Not our problem," said the man with the gun again.

Assessing the situation as he approached, Falcon decided not to interfere as long as they weren't hurting the people. He didn't want to reveal himself until he better understood who the players were. He strolled up the street unhurriedly and stopped in front of the house, watching.

The bag man noticed him first, set down the bag and egg basket, and pulled out a pistol, pointing it at Falcon. "Who are you, and what are you doing carrying a gun in Chester Gordon's city?"

"The name is Falcon. I am looking for somebody."

"He doesn't care why you're here. Only his people are allowed to carry guns. I'm afraid we'll have to take yours."

The second man turned his pistol toward Falcon while the couple scurried into their shabby house.

"You could try," Falcon said with deadly calm, considering whether or not to just kill them. He pulled his pistol and shot the guns from their hands before they could even think to shoot him.

Falcon had decided to use ancient weapons when he came to the West. The modern blaster pistols and ion rifles would mark him as a Federation agent. Locals would be less likely to talk to him if they thought he was from the Fed. They weren't as precise as the arms used in the war, but Falcon had spent time perfecting his technique.

His cyborg enhancements made him faster than the old West's fastest gunslinger, and his aim was dead on. Both men had damage to their gun hands and stood whining and moaning, holding them.

"You will live," Falcon stated. He holstered his weapon and retrieved their guns, sticking them into his cargo pants pockets. "Take me to this, Mr. Chester Gordon. He and I need to have a talk."

"Who the hell are you?" asked the bag man, holding his injured hand.

"Someone you don't want to fuck with." Falcon gripped the man's throat and lifted him, so only his toes touched the ground. "So you can either take me to Gordon, or I can kill you and find him myself."

He squeezed just hard enough to constrict the man's breathing without cutting off his air.

"Cyborg," he rasped.

Falcon slowly let him down and released him.

"You're just one cyborg. You think you can fight a hundred men with guns by yourself?" asked the other man while his friend clutched his throat and gasped.

"I didn't come to fight. I came to talk and look for my female's sister," Falcon stated calmly. He didn't tell them that projectile pistols were not effective against cyborgs. Plus, he had integrated nanite armor that he could activate with a thought that would protect him.

An ion rifle would knock him on his ass and hurt like hell, but it wouldn't kill him. So yes. Falcon could fight a hundred men with guns if he had to, but he wasn't planning on it.

"Come on you two, let's go. Show me the way to Chester Gordon." Falcon jerked his head to the side toward the crumbling road in front of the house."

"What about the stuff we were supposed to collect?"

"Leave it. They said they have children to feed," Falcon ordered.

"And Mr. Gordon has his enforcers and their families to feed."

"Then maybe they should set up gardens and hen houses instead of stealing from people working for what they have."

"It's our fee for protecting them."

"You mean protecting them from the thugs you sent to harass them so they would think they need protection?" He shoved one of them as he walked behind them to hurry them along.

"We didn't do that."

"Of course not. Gordon would have other people do that. The victims will catch on if you send the same people to collect their tribute as those who harassed them."

Falcon didn't tell them things were about to change. He didn't want to tip his hand.

Weshokan was no worse than many other small cities passed over in the bombings. Some buildings were maintained in good condition, while others showed advanced decay. Still, there were many worth restoring if needed.

But Weshokan wasn't the population center it was before the war. Many people died after the infrastructure collapsed from food and medicine shortages. Violence broke out, and people died because the massive destruction left no one to help those who needed help. People unprepared to fend for themselves perished.

Then gangs like Gordon's rose up and took what they wanted from people weaker than they were. Falcon was there to assess the situation and form a plan to get it under control, including how many protectors were needed to do the job.

He could probably manage with four cyborg protectors for this city if there were only a hundred in Gordon's gang.

They had walked almost a mile when they came to an old municipal building. "This is Mr. Gordon's place," one of the wounded men told him.

Falcon scanned the building from his internal computer. He counted three dozen people in various parts of the building. The two thugs he strong-armed were probably telling the truth.

"Leave if you want to live," Falcon told them.

The two scurried away, and Falcon mounted the concrete steps to the front door like he had every right to enter. Of course, he did.

Two guards armed with shotguns stepped out when he reached the platform before the door. They were burly males with long hair and heavy beards. Although they tried, Falcon didn't find them intimidating.

"I need to see Mr. Gordon," Falcon stated.

"Does he want to see you?"

"He will want to know what I have to tell him."

"We will have to take your weapons."

"You can hold them, but I will expect them back when I leave. I've gotten rather fond of my pistol." Falcon pulled out his pistol and handed it to the darker-haired male. Reaching over his shoulder, he pulled the shotgun from its sling and gave it to the other man. They didn't need to know about the pistol in the leg holster or the combat knife strapped to his other leg.

"His office is at the end of the hall. Bert inside will accompany you, and you will wait outside until Bert gives him your request."

Falcon nodded. They didn't need to know that he wouldn't give Mr. Gordon a choice. He didn't want to make trouble until he had to.

Bert was smaller and younger than the other two. He wore a pistol over his right hip. "Follow me."

Falcon followed, walking with the confidence of the apex predator he was. Though he had mellowed some since his war days by removing his emotional dampeners, he had no qualms about asserting himself when necessary.

Chapter Six

Chester Gordon was curious enough about the stranger who walked into his stronghold alone that he agreed to see him. He wasn't alone however, as he sat at a desk facing the door. Two armed guards were flanking him on both sides. One was female, with wild, short-cropped hair and a blue headband around her head. The other was another bearded male.

"I'm Chester Gordon. Who are you, and what brings you into my territory?"

"I'm Falcon Rader, and I have some news that may interest you."

"Oh?"

"Have you heard of the Civil Restoration Enclave of North America?"

Gordon shook his head.

"They were organized before the war, and they made the cyborgs that fought and prepared to re-establish civilization in the case of a catastrophic event. The war ended nine years ago, and the Enclave has reclaimed jurisdiction over this territory."

"I don't think so," said Gordon. "This is *my* territory."

"Only until the cyborg protectors get here. Operations like yours have been shut down all over the old western states. Once they take over, you can no longer live off other people's labor without giving them just compensation."

"What the fuck are you talking about?"

"They are simply re-asserting the laws that governed this continent before the war," Falcon explained calmly.

"The hell you say! Maybe I'll just have Aaron and Jenny blow your head off."

Both guards pumped shells into the chambers of their guns.

Falcon laughed. "That won't stop the cyborg protectors from coming for you in just a few days."

"I don't want to hear anymore... Blast him, guards."

But they were too late. When they pulled the triggers simultaneously, Falcon was already covered in black armor from head to toe. The slugs bounced off without harming him.

Falcon moved at cyborg speed and yanked the shotguns from both guards. He returned to the front of the desk, holding a gun under each arm. His armor receded beneath his clothes, and the three people gawked open-mouthed at him.

"You're one of those cyborgs," Gordon accused.

"I am the cyborg in charge of restoring order to this city and the other cities in the former state of Kansas. I came by to assess the situation and give you prior notice. You will either comply with the law or continue your business on Penta Prison planet."

Gordon's face turned red, and he glared at Falcon, his eyes full of hatred. "What do you get out of it?"

"A place where we can live in peace and raise our families. We can't have thugs stealing produce from families with children. We cyborgs didn't spend our whole lives fighting so thugs could run things on Earth," Falcon sneered the last. "If you don't want to make an honest living, you can be transported east to Overlord territory. Those are your choices. You have a week to decide. One way or another, you will cease these operations."

59

"No machine is going to tell me how to live."

"You have been misinformed. Cyborgs are enhanced humans. I am the chief law enforcement officer for the territory previously designated Kansas and Nebraska. I came to you as a courtesy. When my protector team moves in, you will either comply or be removed," Falcon declared.

"We'll just see about that," Gordon blustered.

"You do not want to fuck with me, Mr. Gordon. You will lose." Falcon backed toward the doorway."

"Female, you are called Jenny? Would that be Jenny Monroe?"

"Why do you want to know?" she asked hostilely.

"Because Raya Monroe wonders if her sister still lives," Falcon said evenly.

"You know Raya?" She sounded hopeful.

"I know her. She still lives on the farm where she was raised. She is well."

"Yes, I am Raya's sister. I meant to go back and see her, but I didn't know if she would still be there."

"She is still working part of the farm. When I return, I will bring a com-tablet for you to speak with her."

"I'd like that," Jenny murmured.

"Be careful who you shoot at. The protectors will shoot back. I don't want Raya's sister to be harmed. It would damage her emotionally."

Jenny nodded.

Falcon offered her shotgun back, and she accepted it. He tossed the other bodyguard his.

"You have one week to decide, Mr. Gordon. More powerful men than you have already fallen."

Falcon turned abruptly and strode from the office. He stopped at the exit to retrieve his guns from the guards. He didn't even have to ask for them. They held them out to him. He took the shotgun, returned it to the sling on his back, then holstered his pistol. Tipping his hat politely, he walked away.

"Falcon! Falcon, wait!" It was Jenny Monroe; he recognized her immediately as he strode down the crumbling road. He stopped and turned to face her running toward him and waited.

"How do you know my sister?" she stopped a few feet from him.

"Raya is my genetic mate." He didn't add that he scanned her as he spoke to determine if she was Raya's sister. She was.

"Your mate? Do cyborgs have mates? Is that the same as a wife?"

"Yes," Falcon replied and waited for her to continue.

"I want to see her."

Falcon looked at her but didn't answer immediately, studying her. He knew Raya cared for the sister she knew ten years ago. Did her sister still care for her, or did she want to hurt her somehow?

He felt certain Raya would want to see Jenny. "All right. Come with me, but I warn you. If you do anything to hurt her, you will answer to me." He resumed walking to where he'd left to sky cycle, scanning the area around him for possible ambushers. He sensed rather than saw Jenny following him.

People watched them as they passed, but no one attacked or accosted them. The couple he'd rescued from the thugs' shakedown came to thank him.

"I am here to protect and serve. I gave Chester Gordon notice. He will either abide by the law of the land or leave. They have a week. They will comply or be removed by my team of cyborg protectors. I will return tomorrow."

"What is your relationship to Gordon?" Falcon asked as they continued toward his stashed sky cycle.

"I am one of his bodyguards. Nothing more. Most of those men know not to mess with me."

"You don't like men?" Falcon wondered.

"I like men just fine, but most of this bunch are bullies or two-faced liars. I can swing either way, but I don't like liars, and I don't like cheaters."

"Yet you work for the mob boss?"

"Self-preservation. Keep your friends close, and your enemies closer. I take care of Mr. Gordon; he takes care of me, and that keeps those assholes that think no means yes from harassing me to fuck them."

"There is an odd kind of logic in that. Now that his organization's days are numbered, what will you do?"

"I'm not stupid enough to fight cyborgs for control of this territory. We were going to find an abandoned farm and settle in when Luke was still alive," she said, keeping pace with him even though she was much shorter.

"You are wise to consider other options."

Falcon thought Raya might have a suggestion, but he wouldn't presume to speak for her. He finally stopped before the old block building where his sky cycle was hidden.

Jenny hung back while he went inside, started, and rode it out.

"Stow your shotgun in this sling and climb on the back. I will fly you back to the farm with me."

"Fly?" She looked at him and his craft uncertainly.

"We don't have time to walk. This will get us there in thirty minutes."

Jenny nodded and did as told. She climbed on behind him and sat back as far from him as possible, so she wasn't touching him. When she was settled, Falcon engaged the cockpit and extended the wings from the bottom. A safety net expanded over Jenny and fastened her in.

The craft rose into the air, pivoted southeast, and shot off toward the horizon.

While in the air, Falcon sent a text to Raya's com-tablet that he was on his way back with a guest. His DNA scan indicated Jenny was Raya's blood relative, but he wanted his mate to confirm that.

Chapter Seven

Flying toward the new home he was making with Raya, Falcon wished he was going alone. He knew it was selfish, but he wanted Raya to himself... To renew their bond by breeding with her hard and then slowly and tenderly.

Bringing her long-lost sister home with him would have them talking for hours. There would be little time alone for bonding with his mate. He sighed quietly to himself; he could wait. Giving Raya her sister back would hopefully make her happy and soothe the emotional damage of all their years apart.

He would do anything for her, including defending her to his death.

Raya came out to the porch when he landed the cycle in the yard. She frowned at the woman sitting behind him. Falcon swung his leg over the steering bar and strode to meet her, taking her into his arms for a brief but heartfelt kiss.

"Who is she?" Raya asked, leaning to the side to get a better look.

Falcon smiled, pleased at the hint of jealousy in her tone. "Come meet her." He put an arm around her shoulders and drew her across the grass to where Jenny sat watching them.

"Hello, Raya," Jenny said with a cautious smile. "It's been a long time." She climbed off the cycle and stood.

Raya gave a low cry. "Jenny! Omigod!" She made the first move, embracing her sister in a fervent hug, crying. "I never thought I would see you again."

Jenny hugged her back, sniffling. "I'm sorry, I always meant to come back... Mom and Dad?"

Raya shook her head. "They died five years ago. Their graves are on the other side of the pasture."

"What about Luke?"

It was Jenny's turn to shake her head. "They killed him days after we got to Weshokan. For a while, I wished they had killed me too." The cold dark anger in Jenny's eyes kept Raya from asking. "It took some time, but I got all the ones who did it. None of them mess with me anymore."

67

Raya studied her sister with a combination of pity and compassion. Falcon didn't find it hard to imagine what those brutal men would have done once she was alone with no one to help her.

"Luke was stupid to think life would be better in the city than here." Jenny withdrew from Raya and let her arms drop to her sides. "And I was stupid to follow him. The two of us were easy marks, riding into town alone."

"I'm so sorry it went badly for you. Unless you have a reason, you don't have to go back. I'm not using most of our family's farm. Pick yourself a spot and build yourself a home."

"I can source materials from the Enclave, and they might even send people to build it for you if you agree to help," Falcon said.

"I don't know what I want to do yet. I just knew when Falcon said he knew you, I had to see you," Jenny said.

Raya smiled at her. "No pressure. I just want you to know this is your home, too. Supper is almost ready. Why don't we go inside and get some cold tea while it finishes cooking."

Jenny nodded her agreement. "That sounds nice. It's been a hell of a day."

Once they were inside with glasses of cold tea, Falcon asked, "What do you think Chester Gordon will do?"

"I don't know, but he was spitting mad. After what you did in his office, he would be stupid to resist the cyborg protectors," Jenny said. "Just so you know, I never collected for their protection business. The deal was I protected Gordon, and his thugs left me the hell alone. I saved his ass when some of his gangers thought they'd take him out and take over his business.

Truth is, I can't stand the motherfucker. I probably can't go back because he will get word that I left with you."

"Your room is still here, pretty much the way you left it. I want you to stay here until you figure out what you want to do," Raya insisted.

"Won't that be awkward for you and him with me hanging around?" Jenny asked, sipping from her glass.

"We've got Mom and Dad's old suite. So that shouldn't be a problem."

"How long have you been together?" asked Jenny.

"Since last month. I signed up to be DNA matched to a cyborg. And Falcon is my mate."

"Just like that, you let a stranger into your life?" Jenny sounded outraged.

"It's not as crazy as it sounds, Jenny. You have to understand. Before Falcon, I lived here for five years alone. …with no prospects for a husband or family."

Raya went on to explain to her sister how cyborgs are programmed to love only one genetic mate their whole life. Even though it had only been a month, they cared for each other and committed to building a life together.

"Now that you put it that way, it sounds okay. I don't know if that would be for me, though," Jenny said.

"You just got here. You don't have to decide anything right now," Raya told her. "Just take some time. Walk the land, take a ride on Suzy."

"You still have Suzy?"

"I sure do. She's in good shape for twenty."

"I can get some nanites to ensure your horse remains in good health," Falcon suggested.

"What will that do?"

"They will repair organ damage, arthritis, and slow aging," he explained.

"If you can, that would be wonderful. Suzy is like part of the family. Wish you could have been here before my dog Monty died. But that was almost two years ago. Haven't had any strays show up or heard of anybody with pups. ...probably because I don't go anywhere, I don't have to." Raya finished her tea and set her glass on the kitchen table at one of the three places set.

"Dinner should be finished. Go ahead and sit while I take it out of the oven."

"Do you need me to do anything?" Jenny asked.

"No, go ahead and sit. It's all in one pot, chicken and vegetables."

Raya carried the pot from the oven to the table with handmade pot holders and set it on an iron trivet in the center of the table. She hardly needed to cut the chicken because it was falling off the bones. She served Jenny a leg and thigh, then queried Falcon on his preference.

Falcon had no preference and told her to pick what she wanted. She took the other leg and thigh and gave him white meat.

The three chatted amiably throughout the meal. As they finished, Falcon said, "If you wish to spend some private time with your sister, I can take the flyer out for some recon."

Raya looked at him with a slight frown. "Will you be back tonight?"

Falcon smiled at her and reached up to caress her cheek. "It should only take a few hours. The flyer is much faster than the bike. I only took that today because I wanted to slip into the city quietly to reconnoiter. Now I will make myself known."

"You be careful out there. I've gotten to like having you around." Raya turned her face and kissed his palm, uncaring that Jenny was watching.

Falcon stood to leave, and Raya got up, too. "I'll walk you out. Be back in a minute, Jen."

They crossed the yard in silence and stopped outside the flyer. "You didn't have to come out."

Raya stepped up to him and put her arms around his neck. "Yes, I did... So, I could do this." She raised up on her toes and pulled his head down to kiss him, pressing her breasts against his chest.

Falcon needed little encouragement to deepen the kiss and hug her in his arms.

"I missed you today," Raya whispered when they ended the kiss. "You be careful out there," she repeated. "Thank you for bringing Jenny home. I'll see you when you get back."

"I look forward to breeding with you, long and slow."

"Me, too." She smiled at him, blushing, then started walking back to the house.

Jenny was smiling as her when she returned to the kitchen. "You're falling in love with him."

"Were you spying on me?" Raya teased.

Jenny nodded, still smiling. "You should have seen him in action today. I'm pretty sure he scared the shit out of Chester Gordon."

"Let's get some more tea, and you can tell me all about it.

Falcon had formed his plan only seconds before they'd finished eating. His first stop was Nelson Waters farm. He set the flyer down a safe distance from the farmhouse, got out, and crossed the overgrown lawn to the front door. He wasn't surprised when that door opened before he reached it, and he was greeted by a man with a shotgun.

"Who are you, and what do you want?"

"Are you Nelson Waters?"

"Who wants to know?"

"I'm Cyborg Ranger Falcon Rader from the Federation Enclave. I came to inform you that Raya Monroe is my mate. I am told you have been encroaching on her land… Using it without permission or compensation. I'm here to see how you plan to remedy the situation. Raya seemed to think that you expected sexual favors in return for consideration of payment for using her land.

That's never going to happen." Falcon rested his hands over his hipbones, looking intimidating with barely any effort."

"Oh, I didn't mean anything by it. I was just trying to get a rise from her, but she wouldn't give me the time of day," Waters hedged. "Ranger, I apologize if I offended her. She is an attractive woman, and I wanted to be with her. She refused, so I took 'no' for an answer."

"A wise move," Falcon agreed. "So, what do you propose in exchange for using her land?"

Waters frowned thoughtfully without saying anything for a solid minute. "Well, how about 10% of the wheat crop I have planted on the 50 acres I use?"

Falcon looked at him thoughtfully but didn't reply immediately. Such a deal could yield almost 200 bushels of wheat depending on the growing conditions. He wasn't quite sure what they might do with that much, plus he knew Raya would not have used the land anyway. Yet he didn't want to make it too easy for Waters.

"I think since this is Raya's land, she should be the one to accept or reject your offer. I will relay it to her and get back to you."

"No hurry. The crop won't be ready for another month and a half. I'm not going anywhere." Waters studied him thoughtfully. "You're one of those cyborgs who fought the war on other planets?"

"I am. I came back to Earth to help put things back in order so we could rebuild civilization. But mainly, I came back to find my genetic mate, the mate I was promised for fighting the war. She is Raya."

"Dang! She was the last single woman in this part of the country. Now, I don't know where I will find a wife."

"When I return to give you Raya's answer, I will bring you a com-tablet. You can contact a service with a list of females looking for mates."

"Thanks, Ranger. I appreciate it."

Falcon tipped his hat. "I'll see you in a few days and bring that com-tablet along with Raya's answer." And with that, he turned and walked to his flyer.

Chapter Eight

Raya and Jenny talked for most of the hours that Falcon was gone. After putting the kitchen back in order, they went out to see their parents' graves. Raya showed Jenny her whole operation, which consisted of the goats, chickens, a horse, and a large produce garden.

"Waters has been running cattle and planting in some of our north fields, but he doesn't think he should have to compensate me for it."

"That asshole could at least give you some beef," said Jenny.

"It would be a nice change from chicken or goat. I don't like killing them, but I don't need more than one buck, and I can't just neuter them and keep them as pets."

"If that's the worst you ever have to do, it's not so bad. I've killed people... Mostly bad people... We had it good here growing up. Weshokan is like a ghost town. Even though they never got bombed, what happened in the rest of the world affected them. I've been in houses that still have decayed bodies in them. Hundreds of businesses looted and abandoned… probably since the first year after the bombs," Jenny lamented. "Going there with Luke was stupid. We were totally feckless." Jenny shook her head as they sat on a bench in the front yard.

"There were five of them with guns. They surrounded us and pulled us off our horses. The bastards beat Luke, tied him up, and made him watch while they took turns raping me. Then they killed him in front of me… Stuck a huge knife in his chest."

"Omigod, Jenny!" Raya cried, tears streaming down her face.

"Yeah, don't cry, Raya. I cried enough for both of us back then. But I finally got away, and some women helped me. One of them, Opal was a martial artist. She taught the women in their little colony how to defend themselves, and me too. Even Gordon's gangers didn't mess with them.

They wanted me to stay with them. Sometimes, I wish I had, but I was hell-bent on revenge. I stalked them and killed every one of them."

"Did it help?"

"Nothing helped. Those men who attacked us were Gordon's, but they acted independently. They stole our horses and used us for entertainment. The nightmares don't come so much anymore. Most of the time, I just feel dead inside.

"Opal tried to help me find peace. For a while, I thought I could. I really loved her, but I couldn't let go of my need to make those bastards pay. After I killed them, I couldn't go back to her.

"I only went to work for Chester Gordon to keep his gangers off my back. When Falcon showed up and took our guns after we shot him....."

"What? You shot my Falcon?"

"Relax, Raya. Did he look like he was hurt to you?"

"No," Raya said finally and frowned.

"He had some kind of armor under his clothes. It stopped the slugs. You didn't notice because his shirt had only two small holes. If we'd used birdshot, there would have been more. But it didn't hurt him. Now that I know he's your man, I'm glad we didn't hurt him."

"So am I. Now that you are out of a job, have you thought about what you want to do?" Raya wondered.

"I'm going to do what you said. Walk the land, and ride the horse. Help you with chores... I need to take my time and figure out what I want. Right now, it feels good to be home."

When Falcon's flyer returned a few minutes later, Jenny took that as her cue to make herself scarce. She disappeared into the house as Falcon emerged from his vehicle.

Raya looked him over in the fading light for any signs of injury as she approached and went into his arms. She murmured his name just before his lips claimed hers in a passionate kiss. It was so good to hold him again, and it scared her a little how quickly he'd come to mean so much to her.

Falcon may not have told her everything about himself, but he never hid his feelings about her. They kissed for a long time before Raya could speak again.

"I'm glad you're back," she told him. "Did your recon go all right?"

"Only one other city I checked tonight has a ganger problem. The others are run by the citizens. I don't think we'll have problems getting control of the others. I'll go out again tomorrow.... But before we go inside, I brought you something."

Falcon went back, opened the door of his flyer, and something whimpered. He picked it up and turned to Raya, holding it in both hands.

"A puppy! You brought me a puppy." Raya held out her hands to take it from him. "The poor little thing is practically skin and bones."

"I found him on the street in the city. When I asked around, everyone just said he was a stray. I didn't think you would want me to leave him there." He grinned at her.

"Of course not. We needed a dog here; he looks like a good farm dog. Thank you, Falcon." She held the puppy under one arm and hugged him with the other. "Well, obviously, he's not housebroken, so we'd better put him in the barn for now. Then I'll find him something to eat."

"I gave him a bolus of nanite in case he had parasites or other ailments, and I got some beef jerky for him to eat for now."

"Great. Right now, I want to get him the leftovers, too. They will help fill his belly and he can take is time chewing on the jerky."

"And then I want to go back inside and get us naked," Falcon whispered.

Raya giggled like a teenager, and they walked to the barn together and put the puppy in a stall. Then they walked into the house, and Raya gathered up some food scraps for the puppy.

"By the way," said Falcon. "I stopped to see your neighbor, Nelson Waters, to discuss how he should compensate you for using your land."

"And what did he say?" Asked Raya.

Falcon explained what they had discussed and told Waters it was up to Raya to accept or refuse the offer.

"It seems perfectly reasonable to me," Raya replied after he had finished explaining. "I probably would have accepted any reasonable offer he made, but he didn't make one."

"Do you want me to stop by and relay that information to him or would you like me to take you there so you can talk to him yourself?"

"You can just tell him. I don't even want to talk to him."

"I'll take care of it," Falcon assured her as she finished gathering food, water, and dishes for the new puppy.

Falcon walked her back to the barn, and they watched for a few minutes as the puppy gobbled up the food scraps Raya gave him. When it looked like the dog was settled, they returned to the house together and went straight to their room. They wasted no time shedding their clothes.

Falcon lowered her to the bed, so her knees were bent over the end. He had done this before, so she suspected his plan. He was tall enough to kneel between her legs and lean over her to kiss her lips. Raya caressed his head and back as he kissed her, his tongue teasing and caressing hers.

He took his time tasting and caressing her body, eliciting soft sounds of pleasure and arousal as he did. He especially enjoyed

83

stroking and kneading her breasts, teasing her nipples into stiff peaks before he sucked them until Raya writhed with need. He knew those sensations went straight to her clit and made it throb for him.

Sliding two fingers into her wet entrance, he kissed and tasted his way down to her mons, stroking her g-spot. She trembled with arousal when his lips closed over her clit, and he flicked his tongue back and forth over it.

Falcon put her legs over his shoulders, holding her down with an arm across her hips as he worked her pussy. Raya whimpered and moaned in ecstasy as a shattering orgasm shook her body, emanating from powerful contractions of her womb. He sweetly teased her through it, making it last as long as possible.

When it finished, he took his fingers out of her and licked them clean. Kissing her pussy, he put her legs down, and laid his cheek against her belly. Momentarily, he stood and lifted her, moving her to the bed's center.

She would have taken him any way he wanted, and she had, but he seemed to like her under him the best, so he could watch her face as he fucked her. Even better, she could watch his face.

Raya quickly discovered cyborgs were not just super soldiers; they were super lovers. He meant exactly that when he said he would breed her long and slow.

She smiled up at him tenderly as he knelt between her legs and lowered himself over her. Drawing her legs up, she welcomed him into her arms as he settled his hips between them and slid his cock into her.

Falcon laid against her, thrusting in and out of her with slow, hard, deliberate strokes. Lacing his fingers through hers, he held her hands against the bed beside her head. When he looked into her eyes with such passion and devotion, Raya wanted to give him nothing less than complete surrender. Her whole body felt quivery, with continuous ripples of pleasure flowing through her.

"I am yours, my Falcon, and you are mine," she whispered. "And I love you." She never believed it could happen this fast. Because she knew taking a cyborg mate was a lifetime commitment, she went all in.

He dropped a light kiss on her lips. "I am yours, my Raya, and you are mine."

He kept fucking her slowly until he sensed she was about to come, then stopped like he had that time before. Raya whimpered and panted, shaking with need.

"Patience, my mate." He soothed, kissing her tenderly.

He took her to the brink a couple more times before he relented and took them both to climax. Raya called his name several times as she came long and hard, his hot nanite-laden seed surging against her womb.

"Omigod, Falcon. That was so good."

He smiled, looking pleased with himself as well as satiated. He'd released her hands, cradled her face between his, and kissed her.

Raya reached down and pressed her hands against his tight ass with him still inside her. He was, beyond a doubt, the best thing that had ever happened to her.

Chapter Nine

The next morning Jenny went to the barn to check on the horse and goats and let them out. Raya had gone to the garden as usual, but she could hear the puppy yipping from the barn when her sister entered.

After letting the animals out into the pasture, Jenny carried the puppy outside. "Hey, Raya, when did we get a dog?"

"Oh, I forgot to tell you. Falcon brought him last night, and I put him in the barn so he wouldn't pee on the floor in the house."

"He's really cute and not very old. He looks like a dog we used to have when we were kids. What did we call him?" Jenny asked.

"Um, Fergus. He kind of looks like Fergus. That's as good a name as any."

"Yeah, I like Fergus. He does look like a kind of stock dog."

"I thought so too. Falcon said he found him in the city on the street. So, he could be anything as far as breed goes. He's a dog. I said I wanted one, so Falcon brought me a dog."

Jenny was still holding the puppy and petting it. "Do you still have our old dog food recipe?"

"I do, but Falcon is having dog food brought in by drone in a day or two."

Falcon was busy the following days doing recon on the other cities and towns in his jurisdiction. More were autonomously run by the residents than mob dictators, which made his job somewhat easier.

Despite his duties, he returned to Raya every night, though not always in time for supper. Somewhere in his travels, he found dog food from a plant near Chicago.

Jenny helped her sister with the daily chores, giving Raya time to show her how to use the new com-tablet that Falcon had supplied her. Jenny was still considering a new course for her life now that she was out of a job. She made herself scarce in the evenings when Falcon returned to give Raya and him privacy.

She was happy for Raya. Falcon was clearly devoted to her and Raya to him. With time on her hands in the evenings, Jenny used her tablet to learn about cyborgs and what it was like to be mated to them. After being raped by the gangers who killed Luke, she never thought she would want to be with a man again.

Seeing Raya with Falcon and the tenderness he showed her sparked a long-dead yearning. She could almost see herself with a man like Falcon, a genetic mate who would only love her for the rest of their lives.

How many times since she'd been away had she longed to be home with her family again? Or to be in Luke's arms again. Well, that would never happen.

All she needed was to let her tablet scan her DNA and enter it into the cyborg database. But what if she couldn't go through with it. Falcon had said he never intended to accept rejection from Raya. He doubted there was a cyborg who would.

Jenny decided to wait and think about it some more. One thing she did know was she needed to get her own place. She could build something small and add to it if she needed more room. There were a couple sites that might be suitable. She thought she might check them out the next day after morning chores.

Falcon left early the next morning to meet his protectors, who flew into Weshokan from Chicago to help root out Chester Gordon's gang. His minions had thinned out since they heard what Falcon did at the boss's office.

Someone had asked the cyborg ranger about this Penta Prison. It was nearly a whole planet run by gangs. Inmates were delivered and left to fend for themselves. They were usually scooped up by one gang or another. Some were gang raped and killed the day they arrived.

While working in the garden, Raya thought about things Falcon shared about his interactions with the residents and the gangers. She was doing some weeding and picking vegetables for dinner as she went along the rows.

Jenny was checking the livestock and collecting eggs from the hen house. Raya stopped to pick some fresh green beans when she heard a soft whine that sounded slightly like Falcon's flyer but at a lower pitch.

Soon a fat, oval transport flying a few hundred feet over the treetops passed overhead. Raya recognized it from a vid on her tablet, but she couldn't figure out what it was doing there. The protectors were coming in on sky cycles.

There was not much activity in the sky on any day, so it was noticed when something flew overhead. Once it passed, Raya returned to pulling weeds until she heard it circling back. This time it was moving low to the ground, about a hundred yards from the garden, and coming in fast.

It stopped on the far side of the garden, and two men came out a side door. Raya got a bad feeling and started to run for the house. A burning pain hit her in the back and seemed to light up every nerve in her body, then everything went black.

Jenny walked from behind the hen house in time to see two men carrying her sister into the vehicle. The door slammed shut, and the transporter lifted into the air, shooting off to the West in the sky.

She dropped the basket of eggs, hoping they wouldn't break, and ran to the house as fast as she could. Inside the house, she sprinted to her room to get her com-tablet. Hitting Falcon's icon, he appeared on the screen almost immediately. He would know Jenny wouldn't call without good reason.

"Falcon, they took Raya! Two men. This big flying thing shaped like a watermelon landed by the garden while I was getting eggs. I came around just in time to see two men take her inside. Then it flew away."

"Fucking traffickers!" Falcon growled. "I'll kill them. How long since they left?"

"Less than ten minutes. They were headed West."

"Probably trying to make their quota before they get to San Francisco. They picked the wrong woman to take. I'm going after her. Can you take care of things there?"

"No problem, Falcon. Just get my sister back, and don't get yourself killed doing it. She loves you."

"And I love her…" he said and cut the connection.

As Falcon ran to his flyer, he used his internal computer to tap into the cyborg network to contact fellow ranger Max Steele in the San Francisco megalopolis.

"Max, I need your help. Traffickers on their way west kidnapped my mate Raya. I think they picked her up on a whim when they spotted her from the air… probably to meet their quota for pickup by the slavers." He sent Max some pictures of her for identification.

"When did this happen?"

"Twelve minutes ago. Her sister just called me from the farm. I'm headed your way, trying to find them. Even if I do, I can't do anything until they land. If I fire on them, Raya and their other captives could be hurt."

"They are probably on their way to rendezvous with the alien shuttle coming to get the captives."

Just as Max gave Falcon the landing coordinates, he blew past the kidnapper's lumbering transport going four times their speed. Falcon slowed and banked north to circle back at a much higher altitude. He made a huge circle going miles out of his way to avoid tipping them off.

He slowed his speed to match theirs, staying behind and above them while he scanned their vehicle for nanites he'd shared with Raya through sex and kissing. She was there!

As soon as they landed, he would get her back.

Chapter Ten

"Shadow, traffickers have taken my mate Raya, and I am in pursuit. Can you go down to Raya's farm to check on her sister Jenny to make sure she is alright? I need to be certain the traffickers did not come back and get her."

"Sure, Falcon. Things are pretty quiet around here. A nice little side trip down to Kansas might be fun."

"Watch yourself because Jenny could attack you if she feels threatened. Make sure you wear your ranger hat and identify yourself."

"Will do. Shadow out."

"Falcon out."

As Raya opened her eyes, she realized she was lying on a hard floor with her hands bound behind her back and her feet bound together with zip ties. Her whole body ached, and her head was pounding. She was surrounded by other bodies lying on the floor around her. Some of them were moaning, and a couple were crying.

Momentarily, she remembered the big vehicle that landed in her field by the garden and the two men who got out of it. She knew as soon as they came out that they were after her. Now they had her, and she could not do anything about it.

"Falcon," she whispered longingly. He would come for her; she knew it.

At the slow speed they were flying, reaching the shuttle pad where the kidnappers would rendezvous with the aliens' space shuttle took over half an hour. Falcon used his internal computer to guide his flyer while he stripped off his clothes and summoned his nanite armor. With his armor in place, he holstered two blaster pistols from his weapons rack behind the pilot seat.

When they reached the shuttle pad, Falcon stopped his flyer and hovered midair, searching for a place to land nearby. He found a spot two buildings away and quickly set his craft down. Barely waiting for the door to open, he launched out of his flyer and sprinted to the landing pad holding the transport carrying the abductees.

Max Steele and a team of cyborg protectors were waiting for the alien space shuttle that had just landed. Falcon communicated with Max through the cyborg network. He would apprehend the kidnappers while Max and the other cyborgs captured the alien space shuttle.

With several other hovercrafts arriving with abductees, the landing pad area became chaotic. As Falcon saw more transports arriving, he signaled Max so he could call in more protectors to capture the other kidnappers.

Three people manned the transport carrying Raya.

Falcon stood before the craft, both blasters pointing at the transport windscreen and the driver inside. He motioned for him to exit the vehicle, then zip-cuffed his hands behind him and set him on the ground beside the hovercraft. Holstering his weapons, he ripped open the cargo compartment door and discovered nine other women besides Raya.

Before he could tend to them, he grabbed the other two men by their throats and dragged them onto the tarmac. Shoving them against the craft, he zip-tied their hands behind their backs.

Pulling his combat knife from the sheath strapped to his calf, he returned to the vehicle and began cutting the ties binding Raya. Although he longed to pull Raya into his arms and just hold her, he went to each of the other women first and cut the ties binding them.

"Don't worry; I'm here to help you. I am Cyborg Ranger Falcon Rader. More protectors have been called to help you return home or take you to a safe shelter. I will stay here with you until they arrive."

As soon as he finished freeing the other women, Falcon turned back to Raya and took her into his arms. "Are you hurt, baby?"

"No, I'm OK. I think they just stunned me, and even though I feel a little shaky, I am unhurt." Raya slid her arms around him and hugged him back. "I knew you would come."

"Always."

Jenny was pacing in the kitchen, pausing to look out the window periodically to see if anyone else was coming. She hadn't heard anything from Falcon, but it had only been about thirty minutes. She couldn't expect Falcon to keep her apprised of the situation while he was in pursuit. If anyone could get Raya back, he could.

Just as she was calming down, she heard the whine of some kind of craft. It was a hovercycle like Falcon's. She cursed herself for not bringing her shotgun from her bedroom and ran back to get it. She made sure that it was fully loaded and strode back to the kitchen door with it.

Opening the kitchen door, she raised the gun to her shoulder and aimed it at the man who had just climbed off the hovercycle. He was putting on a white hat with a circled silver star in the middle of the front.

Jenny's mouth dropped open as she watched him stride toward her. She knew immediately he was one of Falcon's cohorts.... And he was gorgeous!

Jenny knew she couldn't hurt him with a slug from her shotgun, but she couldn't make herself lower it.

"Well, hello beautiful," he said with a smile. "Falcon sent me. I am Cyborg Ranger Shadow Hawk. I came to make sure no more traffickers came by. He said he was in pursuit of the men who kidnapped your sister. I can guarantee he won't stop until he gets her back."

As Shadow came closer, his eyes widened, and he sucked in a breath. When he was nearly a foot from the muzzle of her shotgun, Jenny finally found the sense to lower the weapon. "I'm sorry. I wasn't going to shoot you. I'm just a little upset right now."

"Falcon warned me that you would probably greet me with a shotgun. It wouldn't be the first time. Meeting you like this was certainly unexpected, however."

Jenny frowned. With his smile was a look of wonder and happiness. "What did you expect? I am Raya's sister."

"That's not what I meant. I know you are Raya's sister. I didn't expect that you would be my genetic mate."

Understanding dawned in Jenny's eyes. This was why she felt a giddy frisson of attraction as he came close. She never thought she would feel this way again, not since Luke. "I don't know what to say."

"I'm just as surprised as you are. I just expected a quick flit over the countryside to ensure no more bad guys were here." He paused, studying her face. "I can see that you're conflicted."

"After the life, I've had, I'm not sure I'm fit to be anyone's mate, let alone someone's mother. I had that dream once, but some men killed it.... After they killed my mate."

"When did this happen?"

"Not long enough ago for me to forget. I killed every fucking one of them, but I can never get the picture of them stabbing Luke repeatedly out of my mind. They dropped him in the dirt like a piece of trash. He was my best friend."

Shadow gently rested his hand on her shoulder. "I understand that more than you might think. In nearly a hundred years of war, many of our friends were killed before us, and we could do nothing to save them.

"When we were spawned, they programmed us with an avatar of a genetic mate, a single female with whom we could breed and make offspring. She would be the one and only person born to love us. We were supposed to be united with her when the war was finished. But no one ever compiled a database of our genetic mates."

"Yes, I understand that. I researched cyborgs after Falcon gave me the com-tablet to keep in touch with my sister once I leave. It's like I said. I don't know if I can be that for anybody." Jenny's eyes pricked with tears.

"Jenny, it's OK. I know you weren't expecting this. Neither of us was. All I'm asking is for you to give me a chance to get to know you better. If you do that, you will also get to know me, and we can go from there."

Jenny met his gaze and gave him a faint smile, nodding. He was so handsome, and there was such kindness in his midnight blue eyes that she felt a glimmer of hope stirring in her   soul.

Chapter Eleven

Falcon and Raya stayed with the other women from the abductors' vehicle until the cyborg protectors came to sort out who needed to go where. Falcon thanked them for their assistance, then walked Raya with an arm around her shoulders back to where he left his flyer.

"I just realized that this will be your first time in my flyer," said Falcon.

"I'm sure it will be much better than flying on the floor of that damn transport."

Falcon gently squeezed her shoulders and said, "I can guarantee it." He emphasized that with a kiss on her cheek. "I am so glad that you're safe. I was scared out of my mind when Jenny called and said you were kidnapped. I knew it was traffickers immediately. They've been our biggest headache since we started reorganizing law and order here in the west."

"I knew it wouldn't be good when that big craft landed in my field. I just threw down my hoe and started running, never expecting a stun blast. That hurt."

"You should have told me. I would not have minded fucking those ass holes up a bit."

By then, they had reached Falcon's flyer. He opened the door, helped Raya into the passenger seat, and then climbed in himself. Before he sat in the pilot seat, he returned his blasters to his weapons rack and removed the weapons belt.

Raya watched. Her mouth dropped open as Falcon receded his armor into his body and stood stark naked before her. She allowed her eyes to roam over his body freely, smiling at how beautiful he was, even with a few scars. Quickly pulling on his clothing, he shoved his feet into his smart boots, and they formed around his feet without any assistance.

He dropped into the pilot seat and immediately started the engine. He set the flyer into a vertical ascent, turned it toward the east, and sent it streaking across the bright blue sky. Raya thought she would be nervous about flying because she wasn't especially fond of heights. But she found it exhilarating and fun. She especially liked that they had returned to the farm in almost thirty minutes.

Walking across the grass holding Falcon's hand, Raya was surprised to find a hovercycle parked in the front yard.

Falcon saw her concern and said, "Don't worry. I called fellow ranger Shadow Hawk to check that no more traffickers showed up."

They noticed Jenny and Shadow chatting on their lawn bench as he said that. Shadow had his arm resting on the bench behind Jenny.

Jenny came running when she saw them, hugged Raya, and released her. "I am so glad that you are all right. Was it traffickers like you thought?" she asked Falcon.

"Those bastards were abducting women and selling them to alien slavers. The slave ships would take them to some far-off world, most likely in the Mesaarkan Empire, and auction them off. Apparently, they like human women as sex slaves."

"Ew! I saw pictures of them when I was reading about the war. I can't even imagine, and I have seen some pretty bad things. I am glad you got to Raya before they could put her on some spaceship." Jenny shook herself.

Raya was frowning slightly as she looked over at Shadow, still sitting on the bench. "What's going on with you and the ranger over there?"

Jenny blushed. "Well, um, it seems that Shadow Hawk is my genetic mate." She said the last like she could hardly believe it.

Raya didn't ask her anything else. After what happened to Luke when they got to the city, she knew her sister would have trouble letting herself care for another man, even if he were a cyborg.

"We were just getting to know each other a bit. Shadow understands I have a past I need to make peace with to move forward with a new relationship. He's agreed that we can take it slow. It's not the same as you and Falcon. You asked for a cyborg, mate; I didn't. But now that he is here, it seems like he is too good to pass up."

"In the meantime, you can stay here as long as you want."

"Well, I've been thinking I would like to build that house we talked about … Down by the pond where we used to catch pollywogs."

Raya glanced over at Shadow, sitting on the bench, knowing that he could hear everything even though they were quite a distance from him. He was a cyborg, after all. "What if you decide to accept him?"

"Well, I will still want to visit. I really just want you guys to have your privacy." Jenny looked over at Shadow, feeling butterflies fluttering in her stomach. She was torn between wanting him to go back to where he came from and never wanting him to leave. She needed time alone to think, knowing the pheromones in play were part of what was clouding her judgment.

"Jenny, why don't you ask him to give you a few days and tell him you will call him after you have had time to think about how this relationship could work out for you."

Jenny nodded. "I think that's what I will do." She gave Raya a look that told her Jenny might have said more had Falcon not been standing there with his arm around her.

Falcon and Shadow were friends, but it didn't matter because the other cyborgs hearing had already let him hear everything that had been said.

"Okay, we'll go into the house to give you two privacy. I want to freshen up anyway."

Inside the house alone together, Falcon used the opportunity to take Raya into his arms, kissing her slowly and thoroughly.

"Do you have to go back to Weshokan today?" Raya wondered when their kissing ended.

"No, it can wait until tomorrow. The protectors have all the gangers rounded up. Those who don't want to abide by the law go to jail."

"Good. I just need to be with you right now. I can share you tomorrow." Raya hugged him tighter and laid her head on his shoulder.

"Anything you need. I would do anything for you, Raya. In my old life, I would have killed those bastards on the spot for taking you. Things are different now. Sending them to the mines on Penta Prison planet will be much worse than the quick death I would have given them."

Raya started to cry. "I thought I would never see you again…. When I realized what was happening...." She sobbed against his shoulder.

Falcon held her rubbing her back and stroking her hair, knowing it was good to let her cry it out. He hated that he wasn't here to stop them, that they damaged his mate in their attempt to take her from him and the home she loved.

Yes, killing them quickly was more than they deserved. They were doing evil, kidnapping women to sell to aliens as slaves who would most likely be sexually abused. They would go to a private auction house or be sold to individuals or exotic alien brothels.

If Raya had been taken from Earth, he would have gotten a spaceship, traversed the galaxy until he found her, and ended those who abused her.

Falcon couldn't bear to think of never seeing Raya again.... Never holding her.... Never breeding her.... Never sharing a meal... or helping her with chores again.

He loved her more than his own life. He loved her enough to let her cry in his arms because that's what she needed.

When her tears were finished, she looked up at him. "I'm sorry. I just love you so much."

"And I love you, Raya… always have …always will. You don't have to be sorry. I understand your fear. Losing you is the one thing that terrifies me above all else."

"Me, too." She wiped the tears from her face and then pulled down his head to kiss him again. When his lips met hers, she slipped her tongue into his mouth and leaned into him, her arms wound around his neck. As she ground her belly against the erection that started when he took her into his arms, Falcon knew exactly what she wanted.

Reaching down, he gripped her upper thigh and helped her wrap her legs around his waist, then he headed for the bedroom to help her stop thinking about her ordeal. So, he would stop thinking about it, too, at least for a while.

He kissed and caressed her for a long time before he took her three times, once tender and slow and two more times hard and fast. Afterward, she fell asleep in his arms, and Falcon held her all night.

Chapter Twelve

"Will you be okay today while I finish in Weshokan?" Falcon asked at breakfast the next morning.

"I think so. Jenny is still here, and you said they stepped up surveillance on air traffic coming from overlord territory."

"But...?"

She could tell by his look he knew she was avoiding something.

"What happened yesterday will bother me for a while. I don't want to be clingy about it. I hate feeling like this. I just wish you didn't have to go."

"If I hadn't made this commitment, I wouldn't. I'm calling a protector to come and stand watch while I am gone," Falcon said gently. "I want to be sure you are safe. I will call you later."

Raya nodded.

"Protectors are assigned to most of the towns. I just need a few more days to finish securing Weshokan." He reached across the table, took her hand, and brought it to his lips. "Soon, my duties will be primarily administrative, and the protectors will patrol and maintain order. Then I won't have to do it."

"I will be fine," Raya insisted. "I am just feeling needy because of what happened. Between your protector and Jenny, I'm sure I will be safe."

"The nanites you accumulate from our breeding will help balance your brain chemistry. Hopefully, they will help you cope better with the shock and distress of the last few days." He gave her a sexy smirk. "I will add to them when I return this evening."

Raya smiled affectionately. "Oh, I will look forward to it." She blushed even as she said it. "I love you."

Those three words warmed his soul; he would never get tired of hearing her say them. He kissed her hand again. "And I love you… I always will."

Resigned to spending the day without him, Raya walked Falcon to his flyer. They shared a heartfelt kiss, then she moved a safe distance away as he went inside. She watched as he started the engine and took it up above the treetops before sending it off toward the horizon at high speed. She watched until it was out of sight, then she went to the garden shed and took out her hoe, some baskets, a sunhat, and leather gloves.

Raya came out of the shed and saw Jenny coming from the hen house with an egg basket on her arm. "Hey there. How are you doing?"

"I feel a little needy today. I wanted to curl up in Falcon's arms and stay there all day. But he has his job, and I have mine," Raya admitted.

"Aw, honey. It's no wonder you're feeling a little shaky today. You never had to deal with anything like that before. I'll just put these eggs in the shed and come help you."

Raya waited while her sister took the eggs into the shed to keep them in the shade and returned. "Do you want to weed or pick the fruit and vegetables that are ready?"

Jenny grinned. "You know I hate weeding. I'll pick; you weed."

The two women had only been working for about ten minutes when a hovercycle flew in and settled nearby. Raya could see by the look on Jenny's face that she probably hoped it was Shadow.

"Falcon sent a protector to keep watch so I would feel safer. He didn't think there would be a problem. I know he just did it so I would feel better." They watched as the big cyborg climbed off his hovercycle and approached them. He was armed with a blaster and an ion rifle slung over his shoulder by its strap.

He came to the garden's edge and said, "I am Crocker Mace. I will be your protector today."

"Hello. Do you prefer to be called Crocker or Mace?" asked Raya.

"Just call me Mace. We will not need to interact unless you need something." With that, he walked away to start walking the perimeter of their yard. He did this all day until Falcon returned.

"You were hoping that was Shadow, weren't you?" asked Raya.

Jenny sighed. "Yeah. I wasn't sure I wanted to see him again until I saw the sky cycle and realized I wanted it to be Shadow."

"What does that tell you?"

"That I should call him." She sighed ruefully. "I will call him later after Falcon comes home. That's when I know you want to be alone with him."

Raya smiled at her sister, and they returned to working in the garden.

Jenny did call him and then started packing, not that there was that much accumulated in the few weeks that she had been there. She said her goodbyes and left after breakfast three days later when Shadow came to pick her up.

Falcon returned after dark after calling Raya to tell her he would be late.

Chapter Thirteen

Once inside the bedroom, Falcon closed the door with Raya still wrapped around him. He stood there for a long time, just holding and kissing her---deeply and tenderly, cuddling her in his arms.

Falcon could kiss her for hours, and sometimes he did; at least, it seemed like hours.

He finally set her on her feet and started undressing them. Going back and forth between them, he took her shirt off over her head, then his own. He unwrapped her breasts from her makeshift bra, then knelt before her to worship them with his lips, tongue, and hands.

Raya caressed his head and shoulders, alternately running her fingers through his short hair. She moaned softly and murmured his name at the pleasurable sensations streaking to her core.

She no longer grew impatient with his thorough exploration of her body before he

116

ever put his cock in her. Often, he would bring her to orgasm with his kisses and caresses alone. He did this time too.

More than once, she'd thought irreverently that whoever brainwashed these cyborgs on mating had turned them into fantastic lovers. Under his hand, Raya could easily forget everything but how good he made her feel and how much she had come to love him.

While suckling her nipples, Falcon unfastened her pants and pushed them to the floor. Finishing with her breasts, he kissed and tasted his way down her belly to her sex and kissed her mons. Pausing to slip off her shoes and help her remove her pants, he returned to her pussy and parted her outer lips to tease her clit with his tongue.

Raya jerked at the delightful sensation it sent through her. She sighed blissfully when Falcon set her on the edge of the bed's end. She knew she was in for some excruciating pleasure when he pushed up her legs and buried his face between them. He could make her forget her own name when he did that. And he did it so well!

Falcon licked and sucked and penetrated her with his wicked tongue until she screamed his name, and her body seized with the powerful orgasm. He didn't stop tonguing her clit until she pushed him away, too sensitive to take anymore.

Finally, he got to his feet, toed off his boots, and shed his cargo pants. Raya smiled at him as his erection jutted, pointing straight at her. He held his hands out to her and helped her up, pulling her against his naked body.

Raya kissed the middle of his chest and pressed her cheeks against it while he wiped his face with his forearm. Murmuring love words and endearments, he kissed the top of her head. Hugging her a little longer, he scooped her up and carried her to the bedside, depositing her in the middle.

His eyes were dark with passion as he crawled onto the bed after her. Sometimes, when he was too aroused, Falcon would turn her and fuck her hard and fast from behind. All the different ways they pleasured each other were satisfying. But she had come to relish when he took her long and slow, delaying the finale as long as possible.

He pumped in and out of her slowly, his fingers laced through hers, holding her tenderly captive. Watching her face, he paused every few thrusts to rotate his hips and grind his flesh against her clit. He could tell when she was getting close to orgasm from her breathing and heart rate. Often, he could see it in her eyes.

Eventually, he released her hands, kissing and caressing her face, encouraging her to hold on until he reached his limit. In turn, she stroked him lovingly, running her fingers through his hair and rubbing her hands up and down his back. She gasped and sighed shakily as he teased her with his cock.

Falcon smiled when she pressed her hands against his ass, trying to hold him in place while she tried for a little more friction so she could come. Of course, he relented... when he couldn't wait any longer. Pumping in and out of her harder and faster, he took very little time to bring them to a long and powerful mutual orgasm.

There was so much more to their joining than carnal pleasure. Their souls connected through tender kisses, caresses, and words of love. They both felt as though they were soul mates and genetic mates.

Joining their bodies together in love emphasized their oneness of spirit and commitment to building a life together. Giving and receiving pleasure with their bodies was an act of love.

Falcon had fought his whole life to love and be loved. Now that he had it, he knew it was the only thing worth fighting for.

Epilogue:

Falcon's work started to slow considerably about two weeks after clearing Chester Gordon's gang out of Weshokan. It took time for Raya to recover from her kidnapping, but she got past it with Falcon's love and support.

When Raya hadn't heard from Jenny in almost three weeks, she finally called her. All she got back was a text: "Shadow is my fate, and I've accepted it." She took that to mean Jenny was still getting used to the idea that Shadow was her genetic mate.

As the cyborgs got control of the larger towns and especially the cities, many people needed to make a fresh start. She and Falcon talked about what they would do with her idle farmland. He learned that the Enclave could compensate them if they started a small colony of homesteaders.

Raya divided up six hundred acres of the property into 5-to-10-acre plots. Enclave technicians and advisers helped set it up, bringing construction teams to build houses. When everything was ready, they'd brought in potential tenants for tours.

Some people were not interested in completing the work required to run a successful, self-sufficient homestead. Still, it didn't take long to fill all the spots. Once the new residents settled in, they were offered classes in homestead management, food gardening, and raising livestock. Raya even assisted and gave an occasional class herself.

Falcon kept his job, although it became more of an administrative position as the criminal elements were cleared from the cities and towns. This gave him more time at home which delighted Raya. He was happy living a simple life with the woman he loved.

They finished negotiating with Nelson Waters on compensation for his use of her land. Waters threw in a side of beef in addition to 10% of his wheat harvest. Combined with her wheat, Falcon determined it was enough for them to invest in a small flour mill they could share with the rest of the colony.

With all the new people moving into the neighborhood, Nelson Waters found a wife, which made him very happy. While he never became a close friend to Raya and Falcon, they were friendly acquaintances.

Life in southeastern Kansas was good.

Two years later.

The Homestead Village that Falcon and Raya helped plan was thriving. Every homestead was occupied, and their residents were on their way to becoming self-sufficient.

With his territory under control, Falcon had time to enjoy life with Raya. Sometimes she accompanied him when he flew out on patrol, and they would make stops in scenic locations to enjoy nature.

Now that Raya was heavily pregnant with their first child, she could no longer hike through the wilderness trails. Falcon didn't mind at all. He'd seen thousands of sights on hundreds of planets during his tour of duty in the war. A sight he most wanted to see was the woman by his side.

Their first child was a son, and three years later, they had twin girls.

Raya discovered Falcon had been right about sharing his nanites, making her appear younger and quite a bit more youthful. No one would ever believe she thought she looked older than Falcon. By then, it didn't matter because she was completely secure in his love for her.

The End

Thank you for reading Falcon Cyborg Ranger. If you enjoyed it, please leave a review.

If you would like to hear all my latest writing news, sign up for my newsletter here: http://christinemyers.authors.zone/

Facebook

Twitter

Goodreads

Bookbub

Clarissa Lake

Website

Facebook

Twitter

Goodreads

Bookbub

About the Authors

Clarissa Lake grew up watching Star Trek and reading Marvel Comics. She attended science fiction and fantasy conventions, where she met many well-known science fiction authors and attended their readings and discussion panels. They included sci-fi greats Anne McCaffery, CJ Cherry, George RR Martin, Ben Bova, Timothy Zahn, Frederik Pohl, and Orson Scot Card.

While she loves sci-fi, she always thought there should be more romance, so she started writing it hot and steamy.

Christine Myers has been a science fiction fan since seeing the original "Day the Earth Stood Still" at age eight. Her favorite subgenre is science fiction romance with interstellar space travel and a bit of space opera. Among the most influential in her work are the Lazarus Long novels by Robert Heinlein, including "Time Enough for Love" and Marta Randall's "Journey." She loves Star Trek, Firefly, Farscape, and Veteran Cosmic Rockers, the Moody Blues.

After spending years trying to get her work published by traditional publishers, she discovered KDP and became an Indie Author/Publisher. This means she does it all from writing to publishing.

BOOKS BY CHRISTINE MYERS a.k.a. CLARISSA LAKE

THE ALEDAN SERIES

PSION MATES Prequel
The Aledan PSION
OLTARIN
SURVIVING ZEVUS MAR
PSION FACTOR
PSION'S CHILDREN
CALAN

CYBORG AWAKENING SERIES

CYBORG AWAKENINGS Prequel
VYKEN DARK
JOLT SOMBER
TALIA'S CYBORG
AXEL REX

CYBORG RANGER SERIES

BLAZE
DARKEN
STALKER

MAX

A CYBORG FOR CHRISTMAS SERIES

A CYBORG FOR CHRISTMAS Book 1
BREKAR'S CHRISTMAS Book 2

NAROVIAN MATES

DREAM ALIEN
ALIEN COUNTRY
ALIEN ALLIANCES
HER ALIEN CAPTAIN
HER ALIEN TRADER

FARSEEK MERCENARY SERIES

COMMANDER'S MATE
LIEUTENANTS MATE
SAHVIN'S MATE
ARGEN'S MATE
FAIGON'S MATE

FARSEEK WARRIORS

KRAGYN
NARZEK
RORAN

INTERSTELLAR MATCHMAKING

KORJH'S BRIDE

RADER'S BRIDE
JOVEN'S BRIDE

<u>SZEQART PRISON PLANET SERIES</u>
SOLIV FOUR
CORAZ

Printed in Great Britain
by Amazon

21044443R00079